Concord Cunningham Returns

The

Scripture
Sleuth II

By
Mathew Halverson

Concord Cunningham Returns

The
Scripture
Sleuth II

Concord Cunningham Returns: *The Scripture Sleuth 2*
Mathew Halverson

Cover Design by Richard Schaefer
Cover Illustration by Don Stewart

ISBN 1-885904-25-8

PRINTED IN THE UNITED STATES OF AMERICA
by
FOCUS PUBLISHING
Bemidji, Minnesota 56601

For my parents,
Ray and Mary Ellen

Contents

THE ROLLER PLAY

There were plenty of mysteries in the northwestern town of Pine Tops. And there were plenty of people who tried to solve them. But there was only one detective in town who could solve all the mysteries that no one else could. He was a Scripture Sleuth, and his name was Concord Cunningham.

Concord could crack cases that stumped reporters, principals, and the best Pine Tops police detectives. It wasn't surprising that he had become a local celebrity. What did surprise folks was that Concord didn't use a computer, a cell phone, or even a detective kit when he worked on a case. He used his Bible.

No matter what the mystery was, Concord could find a clue in the Bible to help solve it.

As his reputation spread, more and more people called Concord by his nickname, "The Concordance." Just like an actual concordance, Concord knew where certain words, stories, and objects were found in the Bible.

He also knew how boring last year's annual school play had been. Even Principal Ironsides had fallen asleep in the front row of the audience. That's why Concord sighed when his class was dismissed to the school gym to see this year's play.

"I heard they're doing a roller play this year," Charlie Lowman said to Concord as the two friends gathered their books.

"Does that mean what I think it does?" Concord asked.

"Yep," Charlie said. His messy hair bounced as he nodded. "A roller play is acted out like a normal play, except all the actors and actresses are on wheels. Some use roller skates, some use in-line skates, and some use skate boards."

Concord chuckled as he zipped his backpack and slung it over his shoulder. "Principal Ironsides must feel pretty bad about his nap attack during last year's play," Concord said. "He's never allowed anything with wheels in the school."

"Yeah," Charlie agreed. "I guess I'd feel bad, too, if people remembered my snoring more the play."

The two boys laughed as they followed their classmates to the crowded gym. Once inside, they quickly found seats on the bleachers and observed the scene.

The gym had been converted into a roller play theater. Old sheets had been sewn together to make an incredibly wide curtain. The curtain went from one side of the gym to the other, and it hung from a rope that was strung between the gym's two basketball hoops.

Soon the lights dimmed, the actors rolled out, and the first scene's battle was underway. The actors raced around the gym floor, calling out their lines and clashing their swords as they rolled.

The audience loved it. Even Principal Ironsides seemed to be enjoying himself as he sat in the front row.

Then suddenly it happened.

"The curtain is collapsing!" students in the audience shouted at the actors. "Watch out!"

But it was too late. The curtain and its rope had fallen to the ground, and five of the roller soldiers had rolled right into the collapsed curtain. The soldiers completely lost their balance and fell onto their swords. Fortunately, the swords were foam.

The audience roared in laughter, and the rare grin on Principal Ironsides' face quickly changed back to his usual scowl. He rushed onto the gym floor to see if any students were hurt. Only one student was injured: Ryan Swann. He was the star of the play.

After a few minutes, Principal Ironsides quieted the audience and made an announcement.

"I'm sorry to say that Ryan, who's playing General Germ, has sprained his ankle and won't be able to continue," he said. "Since General Germ is the main character, we're going to have to cancel the play for today. Please return to class."

"Bummer," Concord said to Charlie as the entire audience moaned.

"Yeah, big bummer," Charlie agreed. "I thought I was getting out of math class today."

Concord lifted his backpack to his shoulder, and he and Charlie began climbing down the bleachers. A few seconds later, just as they reached the gym floor, Abby Daniels grabbed Concord's wrist.

"C'mon Concord, we need you!" Abby blurted with a frown. Abby was the student director of the roller play.

"What do you mean?" Concord asked.

"This way!" she said as she pulled the slim, sandy-haired boy across the gym. Concord waved goodbye to Charlie and tried to keep up with Abby's quick pace.

"You have to figure out how Rodney did it," Abby said as she marched. She moved so fast that her long brown hair floated behind her.

"Rodney Doomsey?" Concord asked. Rodney was a classmate who had played mean tricks on Pine Tops kids in the past.

"Yes!" Abby snarled. "The drama class spent weeks getting this play ready, and Rodney ruined it!"

"You think Rodney made the curtain fall?" Concord asked.

"I know he did. I just don't know how," Abby said. "Rodney was backstage when the curtain rope snapped. I told Mr. Ironsides all about it, and he's talking to Rodney now. But I'm worried that Rodney is going to get away with it because I can't prove he did it."

Abby led Concord straight to Principal Ironsides and Rodney, who were talking under one of the two basketball hoops. They were close to where the rope had snapped. The husky principal dwarfed Rodney, who was wearing his favorite oversized hockey jersey.

"Cunningham!" Principal Ironsides barked as he noticed the Scripture Sleuth standing beside him. "Did Abby drag you into this?"

"Uh– " Concord began.

"You bet I did!" Abby interrupted. "Has Rodney confessed yet? He deserves to be in detention for the rest of his life!"

Rodney shook his head in disgust. "That curtain collapsed all by itself," he complained. "I was sweeping the floor behind it when it fell."

Mr. Ironsides folded his arms and scowled at Rodney. "What were you doing sweeping the floor during the play?" he asked.

"You gave me broom duty this morning for bringing matches to school, remember?" Rodney replied.

"Hmph," Mr. Ironsides grumbled as he recalled the incident.

Rodney still had the broom. He leaned on it, and his hands were wrapped around the tip of the handle.

"I must say I've done an excellent sweeping job," Rodney boasted. "This gym floor is spotless, except for that huge fallen curtain cluttering everything up."

"Very funny, Rodney," Abby groaned. "I know you made the curtain fall. I saw you come out from behind the cardboard tower two seconds after the curtain went down." She pointed to a tall tower which stood a few feet away. It was part of the play's castle scenery, and it hid the nearby basketball hoop from the audience.

Concord noticed that the rope had snapped directly behind the tower. If Rodney had snapped the rope, he could have done it behind the tower without being seen.

"I know what you're all thinking," Rodney said. "You think that somehow I hid behind the tower and cut the rope. But there's no way I could have done that. The rope was tied to the basketball hoop, which is ten feet up in the air. There's no way up there."

Concord looked around for a ladder or anything that Rodney could have used to climb up to the rope. He saw nothing nearby, and a quick inspection showed that there was nothing hidden in the tower.

"Maybe you climbed the tower," Abby said.

"I couldn't have," Rodney said as he shook his head. "That tower is too flimsy."

Concord walked over to the tower for a closer inspection. It was all cardboard and very flimsy. Rodney was right. There was no way the tower could have supported his weight.

"So you see," Rodney boasted, "even if I was behind the tower, I couldn't have made that curtain fall."

Principal Ironsides began losing interest. "It sounds like we don't know if Rodney did it or not," he said. His scowl tightened. "Abby, you let me know if you get some proof that Rodney ruined your play. Right now, this looks more like an accident or a coincidence or–Hmph!"

Abby moaned as Mr. Ironsides began walking away.

"Thanks, Mr. Ironsides," Rodney said with a phony smile. "Keep doing a great job running our school." Rodney raised his hand to wave goodbye.

As Rodney waved, Concord noticed that Rodney's palm was black. Concord's eyebrow rose in curiosity. Then Concord glanced at the top of the broom handle that Rodney's hand had been covering. The tip of the white broom handle was black, too.

Rodney looked down at the tip of the handle and quickly put his hand back over it.

Concord's eyes opened wide as he began to remember a Bible passage. He dropped his backpack to the ground and pulled out his Bible. He flipped through the pages for a moment, and then he put his finger on a verse.

"Abby, you'd better catch Mr. Ironsides," Concord said. "Rodney did make that curtain fall."

"How can you prove it?" Abby asked.

"With Judges 16:9," The Concordance said. "Rodney was very clever."

How did Rodney make the curtain fall?

Read Judges 16:9 for the clue that Concord gave Abby.

The solution to "The Roller Play" is on page 72.

2

Soccer Ball Surprise

Time was running out on the soccer field. But it wasn't the play clock that was counting down. It was the irrigation schedule.

The school janitor, Mr. Wicks, had waited as long as he could to begin watering the field. The hoses were unrolled, the sprinklers were set, and the valve was going to be thrown open any second.

Concord and his friends knew that the sprinklers were about to start. But their soccer game was tied, and nobody was willing to stop until there was a winner, even if it meant getting wet.

Out of the corner of his eye, Concord saw old Mr. Wicks walking around the maintenance shed to activate the sprinklers. Concord was hoping for just ten more seconds. He had sprinted from one side of the field to the other, and no one was defending him. He was in perfect position for a winning shot, and his teammate had just passed him the ball.

Concord quickly lined up with the goal. He pulled his leg way back, and he thrust it forward with all his strength. His foot approached the ball at the perfect angle, and just as he kicked the ball, splash! A huge stream of water hit his face.

The splash threw Concord off balance, and he kicked the ball wide right of the goal. The spinning ball rolled past the goal and into the distant football field.

All the players scurried for dry ground.

"That's it for me!" Tim Cannon said as he dodged a sprinkler. "Looks like the game's going to end in a tie."

"Yep," another player said. "I guess it's time to hit the showers. Except for Concord, the showers have already hit him."

All the players laughed. Concord laughed, too, as he wiped water off his face.

"Hey!" Tim called out as he scratched his fuzzy head. "Where's my soccer ball?"

The group looked at the distant football field where the ball was last seen rolling. They had been so concerned about dodging the sprinklers that they had forgotten about the ball.

After Concord got the water out of his eyes, he scanned the football field. The ball wasn't there. Concord knew that he had kicked it hard, but he was certain it couldn't have gone all the way across the field.

"Did somebody take it?" Tim asked.

"I doubt it," Concord said, wringing out his shirt. "I only kicked it a few seconds ago. We would have seen somebody coming or going across the field. And there's no place for a person to hide."

"Then where did it go?" Tim asked.

"Let's go find out," Concord said.

Concord, Tim, and a few other curious players made their way around the sprinklers to the football field. They quickly discovered where the ball had gone: it had fallen into a hole.

The hole was about six feet deep, and it was a little wider than the soccer ball. The soccer ball rested at the bottom.

"It looks like Concord scored a hole in one," Tim said.

"I would have rather scored a goal," Concord replied. Then he rubbed his chin as he looked at the hole. "I wonder what this hole is doing here."

Tim looked to his left and pointed to a distant pile of large metal poles. "It looks like the football field is getting new goal posts," he said. Then Tim got down on his knees and stuck his arm in the hole. His arm went down about two feet, but the ball was six feet down.

"How are we going to get my ball out?" Tim asked the group as he rose to his feet.

"The hole is too narrow to climb down," Concord said.

"And nobody has long enough arms to reach the ball," Tim said.

"Let's try using one of those goalpost poles," another player suggested.

"I think they're probably too long and heavy to use," Concord said. "Even if we could lift one up, it wouldn't help us get the ball out.

"Concord's right," Tim said to the group. "But I've got an idea. Let's see who can figure out how to get the ball out of the hole. Whichever soccer team that person is from wins the soccer game that we didn't get to finish."

After some short discussions, the players all agreed.

Players scattered in every direction. Some ran to the edge of the field to look for sticks. Some ran to see if Mr. Wicks had left the maintenance shed unlocked, which he hadn't. And some ran to look in a nearby dumpster for something that might help.

One by one, players came running back with different ideas of how to get the ball out of the hole.

One player had a long stick. He tried to roll the ball up the side of the hole, but it didn't work. The ball kept slipping out from behind the stick.

Another player had a rope. He tied it into a lasso and tried to tighten it around the ball. But every time he tried to pull the rope tight, the ball slipped out.

A few more players came back with ideas, but none of them worked.

Eventually, all the players had tried their ideas, and the ball was still in the bottom of the hole.

"Hey you kids!" Mr. Wicks yelled across the field. "I'm done watering if you want to finish your game now."

Concord looked up and his eyes locked. A smile crawled across his face as he knelt to the ground and ripped open his backpack. He pulled out his Bible and flipped through the pages in the concordance section. After a few seconds, he found the subject he was seeking. Then he chose one of the verses listed under it, and he turned the pages of his Bible to the book of Genesis.

"Oh, great," Tim said. "Now we have our soccer field back, but we still don't have the ball. Maybe we should ask Mr. Wicks if he's got a way to get the ball out."

"I've got a way," Concord said as he tapped his Bible.

"How?" the players all asked at once.

"It's from Genesis 7:17-18," The Concordance said as he jumped to his feet. "We'd better catch Mr. Wicks before he puts that hose away."

How will Concord get the ball out of the hole?

Read Genesis 7:17-18 for the clue that Concord gave the group.

The solution to "Soccer Ball Surprise" is on page 73.

3

THE BOLLYWONK
COOKBOOK

When the Burley twins missed a week
of school, everything was a little more
peaceful. Fewer kids were being tricked
out of their lunch money. Fewer kids were missing stuff from
their lockers. And Principal Ironsides actually had some
time to himself during the school day.

It seemed that all the kids in Pine Tops had been tricked
by the Burley twins at some point in their lives. That is, all
except for one. As a Scripture Sleuth, Concord always found
a Bible verse to defeat the trickery of the Burley twins.

The Burley twins could usually be found on their favorite
bench in front of the school cafeteria. There they could swin-
dle kids out of their lunch money before it was used to buy
lunch.

Sure enough, the Burley twins were back at their bench
the first day after their week-long absence. As Concord
walked toward the cafeteria, he noticed a particularly large
crowd around the muscular, blond twins. He also noticed
that his friend Charlie Lowman was there, so Concord decided to stop and join the crowd.

"The twins sure have a big audience here today,"
Concord said to Charlie. "Do you think everybody missed
them while they were gone?"

"Nope," Charlie answered. "It's meatloaf day in the
cafeteria."

Concord understood. Many kids would avoid the cafeteria's meatloaf at any cost. They'd even listen to latest offer from the Burley twins. Concord, himself, tried to avoid the school meatloaf whenever possible.

Charlie rose to his tiptoes and tried to see through the crowd. "Hey Concord," Charlie said, "can you see what this is about?"

"Nope," Concord said. "But it's probably another--"

"Hello, friends!" Bart Burley yelled out to the crowd as he jumped onto the bench. "My brother Bernie and I have just returned from a week of vacation with our parents. We were sailing around the South Pacific when we discovered an uncharted island. My brother and I found an amazing secret there!" He held up a stack of papers stapled together like a book.

"You figured out how to staple papers together?" a student joked. The crowd giggled.

"This isn't just paper," said Bernie Burley, who jumped onto the bench with his brother. "This is a copy of the Bollywonk Cookbook."

Students in the crowd exchanged curious looks.

"Send a copy to the school's cooks!" Charlie called out. "They need better cookbooks!"

The crowd laughed.

"You wouldn't want the cooks to have this cookbook," Bart said. "This cookbook has recipes for itching powder, sneezing powder, stink bombs, and more! You can learn how to make all kinds of things that kids aren't supposed to know how to make."

Concord moved through the crowd to see if he could get a closer look. As he appeared in the front row, Bernie saw him.

"Look who's interested in the first copy!" Bernie said.

"It's The Concordance himself!"

Concord scratched his cheek as he noticed that the crowd was staring at him.

"Why is it called the Bollywonk Cookbook?" Concord asked.

"I'm glad you asked," Bart said. "While my brother and I were on the island, we decided to take a hike. We went through a thick jungle, over a tall mountain, and under a huge waterfall. Suddenly, we looked through the bushes and saw a small village. As we walked into it, we discovered it was full of island natives."

"The Bollywonks?" Concord asked.

"That's right," said Bernie. "At first they were scared of us because no Bollywonk had ever seen anyone outside of the small Bollywonk tribe. But we all became friends, and as a gesture of friendship they showed us their recipe tree."

"They have a tree that grows recipes?" joked Charlie.

"Not exactly," said Bart. "The recipe tree is a tall palm tree in the middle of their village. Each Bollywonk has carved his or her favorite recipe into it. The Bollywonks gave us permission to copy as many recipes as we wished. We only had a couple hours before we had to return to our parents, so we wrote as quickly as we could. The recipes were long and detailed, but we managed to get enough recipes copied to make this cookbook," Bart said as he held up a cookbook.

"The Bollywonks also gave us permission to share their recipes with others," Bernie said. "And that's why we're here today."

The crowd started to buzz with interest.

"Why do the Bollywonks have recipes for such funny things?" Concord asked.

"They are fun people," Bart replied. "I guess they must

love practical jokes because with this Bollywonk cookbook you can do all kinds."

"So you're giving these recipes away?" Concord asked.

"Almost," Bernie said. "It did cost us money to photocopy the cookbook for everyone. And it was hard work to put the copies together. Still, we've decided to be generous and sell the cookbooks for the very low price of five dollars apiece."

Bernie handed Concord a cookbook. Concord opened the cookbook to inspect the first recipe, which was titled "Super Sneezing Powder." It listed ingredients such as coconut, ground-up feathers, and baked palm leaves. It also gave detailed directions for how to mix them into powder.

"Can't we just get these recipes in the library?" a student called out from the crowd.

"Not these!" Bernie shouted. "These are Bollywonk recipes, and no library will have them."

"Why not?" Charlie asked.

Bernie leaned over to Bart and whispered in his ear. Bart nodded and whispered back.

"Like we said," Bernie said, "nobody had ever found the Bollywonks before we did."

"And," Bernie said, "we don't know if anyone will ever find them again because they live so deep in the jungle. We were lucky to find our way back to our parents."

"Not only that," Bart said, "but our parents don't even know what island we were visiting. They said it wasn't on any map. So you're very lucky you know us because we're the only ones with the Bollywonk's secrets."

Some excited students in the crowd began pulling money out of their pockets.

Concord looked up from the cookbook. His eyes darted to the left and the right, as if he was reading an invisible book. Actually, he was remembering a Bible verse.

Then Concord handed the cookbook back to Bernie. He unzipped his backpack and pulled out his Bible. He turned straight to the book of Acts. After a moment, he looked up at the crowd.

"I'm sorry to report that the Bollywonk cookbook is fake," Concord announced.

"What?" Bart and Bernie said together. "How can you say that?"

"Because of Acts 2:8," The Concordance said as he held his Bible in the air. "I don't think the Burley twins ever met the Bollywonks."

How did Concord know the cookbooks were fake?

Read Acts 2:8 for the clue Concord gave the Burley twins.

The solution to "The Bollywonk Cookbook" is on page 74.

4

THE SASQUATCH
SNAPSHOT

Cookies never lasted long in the Cunningham house. With three kids in the family, Mrs. Cunningham wasn't surprised. What she didn't know was that the real Cunningham cookie monster was Mr. Cunningham. He could finish a plate of cookies before the kids could even pour a glass of milk.

That's why Concord was relieved when the phone rang. He and his dad were just about to share a plate of fresh chocolate chip cookies. As Mr. Cunningham got up to answer the phone, Concord knew that the cookies were all his.

"Sasquatch?" Mr. Cunningham said into the phone.

Concord's hand froze just as he was reaching for his first cookie.

"Okay, I'll be there in a few minutes," Mr. Cunningham said. He hung up the phone and walked back to the table.

"A Sasquatch is a bigfoot, isn't it?" Concord asked.

"Yep," Mr. Cunningham said as he grabbed a cookie. "There's a guy down at the newspaper who is selling some pictures he snapped of a Sasquatch in the forest. My editor wants me to check them out."

As the top reporter for the *Ponderosa Press*, the local newspaper, Mr. Cunningham was always asked to report the most exciting stories.

"Could the pictures be real?" Concord asked.

"I doubt it," the tall reporter answered with his mouth full of cookie. "People have been looking for proof of a Sasquatch for years and have never found anything."

"Didn't somebody claim to have seen one a couple years ago up by Bigwood Lake?" Concord asked.

"Yeah," Mr. Cunningham said as he paused to take a sip of milk. "The supposed Sasquatch turned out to be old Montana Jones. He's a mountain man who hasn't cut his hair in thirty years. We get mistaken sightings of him all the time. In fact, somebody saw him swimming in the Grand Pine River last month and reported seeing a six foot-long beaver."

They chuckled. Concord looked down at the plate of cookies and realized his dad had already eaten half the plate. Concord grabbed one while he still had a chance.

"Dad, I was wondering," Concord began.

Mr. Cunningham knew what his son was going to ask.

"Grab your shoes," Mr. Cunningham said. "You can come with me to check this out." Concord smiled and ran for his shoes. When he got back to the table, his dad was ready to go. And the cookie plate was empty. At least Concord had managed to get one.

When they arrived at the *Ponderosa Press*, they were introduced to the man with the supposed bigfoot pictures, Peter Cutler. He was a bald man wearing a red plaid vest.

"I suppose we should get right to it," Mr. Cutler said. He opened a folder and spread three pictures on the table. Two pictures showed footprints. The other was taken at night, and it was very dark. It showed the gray outline of a human-like form against the darkness.

"Your paper still offers to buy pictures of bigfoot sightings, doesn't it?" Mr. Cutler asked.

"We do unless it's obvious that the pictures are fake," Mr.

Cunningham said. "Otherwise, our readers like to see the evidence and decide for themselves whether or not they're looking at a real bigfoot."

"These are real," Mr. Cutler said with a smirk. "I was camping north of Bigwood Lake. I decided to go on a day hike to shoot some wildlife pictures. A couple miles above my camp I found these footprints."

Mr. Cutler pointed to the footprint pictures and the Cunninghams examined them.

"You'll notice that I put a soda can inside the footprint so you can see how big the foot really is."

"It looks like it's about a size fifty!" Concord exclaimed.

"You're not joking," Mr. Cutler said. "Those footprints went down a dirt trail that doesn't appear on any hiking map. I followed the trail to a creek, and the footprints disappeared there."

"We're usually not interested in footprints," Mr. Cunningham said. "Anyone can dig them out with a spoon or shovel. What about this other picture?" he asked.

"That's the Sasquatch," Mr. Cutler said. "I had decided to hide behind a log at the creek to see if the Sasquatch would come back. It got dark, and I was just about to give up. Then I heard something in the woods, so I decided to wait a little longer."

"Weren't you getting scared?" Concord asked.

"You bet I was," Mr. Cutler said. "To make things worse, a storm was approaching. The dark clouds covered up the rising moon and there was barely enough light to see."

"That's why the picture is so dark," Mr. Cunningham concluded. "Didn't you have a flash on your camera?"

"I did," Mr. Cutler said, "but as I heard the Sasquatch get closer and closer, I became afraid to use the flash. I didn't want to scare the Sasquatch and possibly make him mad at me."

"So what did you do?" Concord asked.

"I decided to take a picture with a really long exposure time," Mr. Cutler replied.

"What does that mean?" Concord asked.

"The exposure time is how long the camera's shutter stays open. The shutter is the little door that lets light onto the film," Mr. Cutler explained. "Usually the shutter stays open only a fraction of a second. Otherwise, too much light comes in and the picture is all white."

"But, since it was really dark, you could leave the shutter open for a long time and the picture wouldn't be ruined," Concord concluded.

"Right," Mr. Cutler said.

"That's the way to do it if you can't use your flash in the dark," Mr. Cunningham agreed.

"My camera has a button that makes the shutter stay open for as long as I hold the button," Mr. Cutler said. "I figured that since there was hardly any light, thirty seconds would be about right."

Mr. Cunningham nodded. "Sounds about right," he said. "So when the bigfoot got in front of the camera, you held the shutter open for about thirty seconds?"

"Almost," Mr. Cutler said. "Fortunately, the bigfoot did stop right in front of me, so I opened the shutter. I held it open as I counted silently in my head."

"So why is the picture still so dark?" Concord asked as he looked at the picture.

"As I said, I didn't quite make it to thirty seconds," Mr. Cutler said with a sigh. "If there only would have been a little more light, the picture would have shown the bigfoot perfectly!"

"Too bad the moon didn't come out from behind the

clouds for a second while the shutter was open," Mr. Cunningham said as he looked at the dark figure on the picture. "It wouldn't have taken much light at all to give us more detail."

"So why weren't you able to hold the shutter open for the full thirty seconds?" Concord asked. "Did the Sasquatch move?"

"Yeah," Mr. Cosgrove said with a sigh. "I was about two-thirds through the thirty seconds of open shutter. Suddenly, a gigantic clap of thunder roared right above us. It was incredibly loud! I think it must have happened within a couple hundred feet of us because my ears are still ringing from it. I guess it really scared the Sasquatch because he ran off. So, I let the shutter close, put my camera away, and headed back for my camp. I went to the camera shop to develop the pictures when I got back to town today, and then I came right over here."

"Well," Mr. Cunningham said, "I think our readers would probably enjoy hearing your story and seeing your picture, even though it's a little dark. Let's see if we can agree on a fair price."

Concord's eyes darted from side to side as he searched his memory. While Mr. Cunningham talked to Mr. Cutler, Concord unzipped his backpack and pulled out his Bible. After a few moments of Scripture sleuthing, Concord tapped his dad on the shoulder.

"I don't think these pictures follow the paper's rules, Dad," Concord said.

"What do you mean?" Mr. Cunningham asked.

"We know the pictures are definitely fake," Concord replied.

"Why do you say that?" Mr. Cutler asked.

"The reason is in Matthew 24:27," The Concordance said. "Mr. Cutler can't be telling the truth."

How did Concord know Mr. Cutler was lying?

Read Matthew 24:27 for the clue that Concord gave to his dad and Mr. Cutler.

The solution to "The Sasquatch Snapshot" is on page 75.

5

SURVIVALIST STICKUP

"Cunningham!" the editor yelled across the newsroom. Mr. Cunningham and Concord were just leaving the *Ponderosa Press*.

The editor hurried across the newsroom to catch them at the door. "We just heard that the police are about to arrest a suspect in yesterday's robbery," he said.

Concord turned to his dad. "Who got robbed?" he asked.

"The last place that anyone would expect to get robbed," Mr. Cunningham said.

Concord thought for a moment. "The police station?" he asked.

Mr. Cunningham raised an eyebrow. "Good point," he said. "Okay, it's the next to last place anyone would expect to get robbed."

Concord thought again.

"The sewage plant?" he asked.

"Oh," Mr. Cunningham said. "Good point, again. Okay, it's the next to next to last--"

"Ah," the editor interrupted, "time is slipping away. The arrest is taking place at 997 Mountain Side Road."

"Right," Mr. Cunningham said. He grabbed his notebook and pen. "C'mon, Concord. I'll tell you on the way."

They were soon driving toward the address, which was on the edge of town.

"Believe it or not, it was the Pine Tops Garbage Dump that got robbed," Mr. Cunningham said to Concord.

"There must be some pretty valuable garbage out there," Concord chuckled.

"This robber got a little bit more than garbage," Mr. Cunningham said. "He robbed the fee collector's booth at the dump's entrance."

"Was there much money there?" Concord asked.

"You bet," Mr. Cunningham said. "People have to pay fees to dump their garbage, and they even pay extra to dump tires and other things. By the end of the day, there were probably hundreds of dollars out there."

The Cunninghams arrived at the address and immediately saw Police Chief Riggins talking to a man with a backpack. The chief asked the man to wait with a deputy on the sidewalk, and then the chief went back to his patrol car to get something.

Mr. Cunningham grabbed his notebook and made his move. Concord followed.

"Good afternoon, Chief Riggins," Mr. Cunningham said.

"Hello, gentlemen," Chief Riggins said. As usual, the chubby police chief wore a freshly pressed uniform, and his mustache was perfectly trimmed. He clicked his cheek twice as he nodded at Concord.

"Is the man on the sidewalk a suspect in yesterday's dump robbery?" Mr. Cunningham asked as he opened his notebook.

"He sure is," Chief Riggins said.

"Why do you think it was him?" Mr. Cunningham asked.

"The man working in the dump's fee collection booth recorded the license plate of the robber's car," the chief said. "The robber had parked a block away, but the dump worker had binoculars in the booth."

"So the worker was able to zoom in on the robber's license plate," Mr. Cunningham concluded.

"Right," the chief said. "We ran the license plate through the system, and the car was registered to this man, Ron Cosgrove."

"Isn't he the wilderness survival instructor at the community center?" Mr. Cunningham asked.

"That's him," the chief said. "When we got here, he was just walking up with a pack on his back."

"So was the money in the backpack?" Concord asked.

"Nope," Chief Riggins answered. "There was only wilderness survival gear in the pack. In fact, Mr. Cosgrove says he's been on a survival trip on Mount Redhead for an entire week. He says he's just now getting home."

"How did he explain his car being used as a getaway car yesterday?" Mr. Cunningham asked.

"He couldn't at first," the chief said. "He looked surprised that his car was involved."

"Maybe the surprise was that you were able to track him down," Mr. Cunningham said.

"That's what I figured, too," the chief said. "Now he says that somebody must have stolen his car and used it in the robbery." The chief sighed. "And I suppose that's possible. He lives here on the edge of town, so he doesn't need a car to go on wilderness survival trips. He just hikes from here through the surrounding trees to the base of Mount Redhead, and away he goes."

"So, if he's telling the truth, he didn't even see his car for a week," Mr. Cunningham concluded.

"Right," Chief Riggins said. "We don't have any other evidence against him, and we can't prove that he's lying about being up in the mountains this past week. Nobody has seen him around town, and his phone records show that his phone hasn't made any calls for eight days."

"Wasn't the booth worker able to identify him?" Mr. Cunningham asked.

"Nope," the chief answered. "The robber was totally disguised, including a ski mask over his face. And, the robber never used his voice. He only held out a sign that told the booth worker to give him all the money."

"Did the robber have a gun?" Mr. Cunningham asked.

The chief shook his head. "He showed a knife," he said. "Mr. Cosgrove just told me I could search his backpack, so I'm going to see if I can find the knife or any other evidence."

Chief Riggins grabbed some plastic evidence bags out of his car and walked back to Mr. Cosgrove. The Cunninghams followed.

As the chief pulled items out of Mr. Cosgrove's backpack, he carefully dropped them into the clear evidence bags. Concord was amazed at how little Mr. Cosgrove had taken on his survival trip. There was a box of matches, a few feet of rope, a small pan, a cup, a couple bandages, some lotion, a jacket, and a hat.

"Chief Riggins," Ron Cosgrove said, "can you give me some of that lotion before you bag it. This sunburn is killing me."

Mr. Cosgrove's face was bright red with sunburn. The chief gave Mr. Cosgrove some lotion, and Mr. Cosgrove rubbed it into his face. It helped right away. His cracked and peeling nose, cheeks, and chin became smooth as silk.

"Thanks," he said. "It's been a sunny week on Mount Redhead."

"Mr. Cosgrove," Mr. Cunningham said, "are you saying that you've been up in the wilderness of Mount Redhead for a week, and you haven't been down off the mountain since you left?"

"That's correct," Mr. Cosgrove said with a nod.

"I noticed that Chief Riggins didn't find a knife in your backpack," Mr. Cunningham said. "I've heard that you're always supposed to take a knife with you in the wilderness. Do you have one in a pocket or somewhere else?"

"Nope," Mr. Cosgrove said. "The chief searched me before you got here." Chief Riggins nodded in agreement. "Besides, it's more of a challenge to survive without a knife," Mr. Cosgrove said. "I'm always looking for a good challenge."

"Did you meet anyone else on your trip?" asked Chief Riggins.

"Nope," Mr. Cosgrove said. "It was just me and Mount Redhead."

Concord looked at all the items in the backpack. Then he opened his own backpack and dug out his Bible. A few minutes later he had his finger on a verse and a question for Mr. Cosgrove. "Mr. Cosgrove, did you take anything else with you besides what's in your backpack?"

"That's everything," Mr. Cosgrove replied. "I lived off the land."

Concord turned to Chief Riggins. "Chief," Concord said, "Mr. Cosgrove's story can't be true."

"Did you see something in the backpack?" Mr. Cunningham asked.

"It's what I didn't see," Concord replied. "Isaiah 7:20 explains it."

How did Concord know that Mr. Cosgrove was lying?

Read Isaiah 7:20 for the clue that Concord gave Chief Riggins.

The solution to "Survivalist Stickup" is on page 76.

6

THE SWEATSHIRT
SWITCHEROO

The bus was just pulling into the youth center parking lot when Concord arrived. His parents had asked him to meet his sister, Charlotte, when she got back from her overnight camping trip.

Concord's spunky, red-headed sister had been looking forward to the camping trip, but not because she liked sleeping in a tent. And not because she wanted get bug bites all over her arms and legs. And not even because she got to go to beautiful Camp Maranatha. It was because her best friend, Becky Rollins, was going.

That's why Concord was so surprised to see the two girls arguing when they stepped off the bus.

"You switched sweatshirts with me!" Charlotte yelled at Becky, tugging at the sweatshirt Becky was wearing.

"Did not, Charlotte!" Becky shouted back. She flung her long black hair over her shoulder. "That one's yours," she said, pointing to the sweatshirt tied around Charlotte's waist.

Concord breathed a deep sigh. He didn't want to get in the middle of the argument. But, his mom and dad had asked him to help Charlotte carry her gear home. That meant he couldn't leave without her.

The two girls stood back to back, both with their arms folded. Concord quickly glanced at the two Camp Maranatha sweatshirts. He decided the girls must have bought them at the camp store. "The sweatshirts look exactly the same to me," Concord said as he approached them, hoping he had just solved the problem.

Charlotte turned to her brother and untied the sweatshirt around her waist. She handed it to him, and he saw what was wrong. The sweatshirt had about fifty small purple stains across the front.

"Oh," Concord said. Then his eyes brightened. "It'll probably wash out. No big deal, Charlotte."

"I can see you're not very good at berry identification," Charlotte said. "Those are huckleberry stains. They probably won't wash out. That's why I'm not going to let Becky switch sweatshirts with me. My sweatshirt is perfectly clean, and she's wearing it!"

"That is your sweatshirt," Becky said, pointing at the stained sweatshirt Concord was holding. "And I'm not going to trade with you just because you're sad that yours is stained."

Concord handed the stained sweatshirt back to Charlotte. "Why do you think that the stained sweatshirt belongs to Becky?" he asked.

"Because we were both sharing a tent with Kelly Rankin," Charlotte said.

Concord raised an eyebrow in confusion.

Charlotte explained, "Kelly had to go to the outhouse in the middle of the night, and she borrowed this sweatshirt when she went."

"But you don't know whose sweatshirt she borrowed?" Concord asked.

"Right," Becky said. "And it wouldn't have mattered, except that Kelly fell into a huckleberry patch on her way to the outhouse. The berries were so ripe that she squished huckleberry juice all over the sweatshirt when she fell into the patch."

"And the two sweatshirts were exactly the same before that?" Concord asked.

"Yes," Charlotte said. "Both sweatshirts were brand new, size medium. We each bought one at the camp store earlier in the day, and we wore them all evening."

"Doesn't Kelly remember where in the tent she grabbed the sweatshirt she borrowed?" Concord asked.

"Nope," Charlotte answered. "She was so sleepy that she barely remembers borrowing it."

"Even if she knew where she grabbed it," Becky added, "we still couldn't be sure whose sweatshirt she grabbed."

"Why not?" Concord asked.

"The tent was kind of messy," Becky said.

"The tent was really messy," Charlotte agreed.

The girls giggled.

"Also, I had to change into my pajamas in the dark last night," Becky explained, "So, I wasn't sure where I put any of my clothes, including my sweatshirt."

"Why didn't you use a flashlight or a lantern when you changed?" Concord questioned.

"Charlotte and Kelly were already asleep," Becky explained, "and I didn't want to wake them. You see, we chose to do different activities last night. The activities ended at different times, so we had different bedtimes. I went on the night hike that the local ranger was leading. Charlotte and Kelly sang songs by the campfire."

"I should have gone on the night hike," Charlotte said. "No matter where I sat, the smoke from the campfire kept following me and making me cough."

"You know what they say about smoke," Becky said. "It always follows--"

"Beauty, of course," Charlotte finished, stroking her hair.

The girls giggled again.

"Anyway, by the time I got back from the night hike," Becky continued, "the campfire was out and Charlotte and Kelly were already in bed."

"So when you both woke up this morning, where were the sweatshirts?" Concord asked.

"They were right next to each other," Charlotte answered. "The only difference between them was that one sweatshirt was stained with huckleberry juice."

Concord stared at the stained sweatshirt. Then his eyes moved from side to side as he considered the night's events. He dropped his backpack to the pavement and pulled out his Bible. He began skimming the topics in the concordance. Before long, he was flipping the pages of his Bible to a verse in Genesis. Once he found it, he looked at the girls.

"I'm not sure whose sweatshirt got stained, but I'll be able to tell you in about five seconds," Concord said.

"How will you know?" Charlotte asked.

"Read Genesis 27:27 and think about what Charlotte did last night," The Concordance said. "You'll be able to tell them apart, too."

How will Concord know whose sweatshirt got stained?

Read Genesis 27:27 for the clue that Concord gave the girls.

The solution to "The Sweatshirt Switcheroo" is on page 77.

7

LOCKER TALK

Concord was always interested in the weather report on school days. While most folks hoped for sunshine, Concord usually hoped for rain. So did the other kids in his gym class. A rainy morning meant that the class would get to play dodge ball in the gym. A sunny morning meant that Mr. Russell, the physical education teacher, would make the class run laps around the school track.

Today's sky was totally blue, and the class was totally bummed. Mr. Russell told the students to lace up their running shoes and meet him outside. A few minutes later, the class was stretching out on the school track.

"Attention class!" Mr. Russell shouted as the students lined up. "Today we're going to do six laps."

The class moaned.

"Don't stop until you finish!" he shouted. "Ready, set, go!"

Concord sprinted from the starting line and was immediately out of breath.

"I do that every time," he said to himself. "I need to pace myself."

He was just finding his stride when Lizzy Rupert jogged up along side him.

"What does the Bible say about tattletales?" Lizzy asked as her blond curls bounced up and down.

Concord slowed his pace a bit and considered the question.

"Hmm. The Bible says you're always supposed to tell the truth," he replied as he exhaled. He drew in a breath for his next sentence. "That's one of the Ten Commandments. They're in Exodus 20." Then he scratched his head. He knew he hadn't really answered Lizzy's question.

"But what about telling on somebody?" she asked again. "And what if it's dangerous?"

"Dangerous?" Concord repeated. He stopped and pulled her off the track. "Did you witness a crime or something?"

"Not yet," she said. "But I know when one is going to happen."

"How do you know?" Concord asked, gasping for a breath as he leaned over and placed his hands on his knees.

"Because I overheard the Burley twins talking at their lockers," she said. "My locker is right next to theirs."

"Uh-oh," Concord said. "Are the twins going to try to sell fake stuff again?"

"No," she said. "But one of them is going to cheat on the social studies test."

Concord curled an eyebrow. "The social studies test was yesterday," he said.

"I know," Lizzy agreed. "But one of the Burley twins, Bart, wasn't in school yesterday. He's going to take the test after school today."

"And you overheard the twins planning how Bart is going to cheat?" Concord asked.

"Yes," Lizzy said.

Mr. Russell's whistle blasted from the other side of the track. "Cunningham! Rupert!" he yelled. "Keep it moving!"

They started jogging again, and Lizzy told Concord what she had overheard.

"They got the idea from Mr. Russell because he always blows that whistle," Lizzy explained. "Do you remember what the social studies test was about?"

"Sure," Concord said. "It was a test about music history. We studied famous songs and when they were written. The test had a list of songs, and we had to the put them in the correct order--from oldest to newest."

"Right," Lizzy confirmed.

Concord thought about what the twins might do. "Did Bernie write down the songs on the test so Bart could memorize their order?" Concord asked.

"They said they tried that," Lizzy said. "But it didn't work. I guess Bart isn't very good at memorizing things. He couldn't keep all the songs straight."

"Is Bernie going to pretend that he's Bart and take the test for him?" Concord asked.

"Nope," Lizzy said. "They thought of that, too. But they think the social studies teacher can tell them apart."

"Then I give up," Concord said as they jogged past Mr. Russell.

"Don't give up, Cunningham!" Mr. Russell shouted. "Only five laps to go. Keep it moving!"

"Yes, sir!" Concord said, speeding up slightly.

Lizzy matched his pace.

"The twins got their idea during their gym class this morning," she explained. "Bernie is going to sneak into the gym after school and borrow Mr. Russell's whistle. Then he's going to take some friends onto the field, near the social studies classroom window. Bart will be inside taking the test, trying to figure what order to put the songs in. While Bernie's friends run around the field, Bernie will pretend to be the referee blowing the whistle. Except, he'll actually be whistling songs with it."

"And he's going to play the songs in the order that they need to be answered on the test," Concord concluded.

"Right!" Lizzy said. "Bart will be able to hear the whistle through the classroom window."

"Won't the teacher hear the whistle, too?" Concord asked.

"She probably will," Lizzy agreed. "But the twins don't think she'd ever notice that Bernie is whistling the order of the songs on the test. She'll probably be working on something else and just think some kids are playing in the field."

"They're probably right about that," Concord said. "But there are fifteen songs on that test. That's a lot of whistling."

"That's true," Lizzy nodded. "But if anybody asks, Bernie's going to say that the whistling is just part of the game his friends are playing."

"And Bernie thinks he remembers all of the songs from the test?" Concord asked.

"I heard him say that he went back over his class notes and picked out the songs that were on the test," Lizzy said. "Then he wrote them in order on a piece of paper. He's going to take the paper out into the field when he whistles. So what do you think, Concord? Should I tell on the Burley twins or not?"

Concord's eyes darted from one side to the other as he considered Lizzy's question. Then he searched his memory for a Bible verse that might hold a clue. He'd been working on memorizing Scripture for situations like this when he didn't have his Bible with him.

Finally, it came to him. "I don't think you need to bother telling on them, Lizzy," Concord said. "They're not going to get away with it."

"How do you know?" Lizzy asked.

"Because of 1 Corinthians 14:7," The Concordance said. "There's something that the Burley twins forgot."

How did Concord know the Burley twin's plan would fail?

Read 1 Corinthians 14:7 for the clue that Concord gave Lizzy.

The solution to "Locker Talk" is on page 78.

8

MURDOCK'S MINE

Concord decided one month was just about right. That's how long his older brother, Cody, had been working in the Pine Tops Ice Cream Parlor. Concord's theory was that after a month, Cody would be able to give him a free cherry cheesecake ice cream cone.

To test the theory, Concord decided to walk down to the ice cream parlor on a sunny Saturday afternoon, just before Cody's shift ended.

"Sure, I'll give you a free cone," his curly-haired brother said, "as long as you mow the lawn for me. Dad's been asking me to do it for days."

"I guess so," Concord agreed. It wasn't a very good deal, but he couldn't resist the cherry cheesecake ice cream.

Cody handed Concord the cone, grabbed one for himself, and then led Concord out to a bench in front of the parlor. The parlor was on the edge of the Pine Tops town square, where there were plenty of people to watch.

"Here comes Chief Riggins," Cody said as he elbowed Concord.

Concord nearly lost the top scoop off his cone from the bump. After balancing his cone, he looked up and saw the chief heading toward the bank.

"Hey, Chief! Is somebody robbing the bank?" Cody asked with chuckle.

"Not the bank," the chief said, briefly stopping to talk to the boys, "but maybe Murdock's Mine."

"Murdock's Mine?" Cody questioned. Then he shook his head. "That's just a myth."

"Maybe so," the chief said. "But I just got a call from the bank. A man is there with twenty pounds of gold nuggets. He says he got the gold from Murdock's Mine, and he wants to cash it in."

"What's Murdock's Mine?" Concord asked.

"It's an old gold mine that is supposed to be in the mountains north of here," Cody said. "I learned about it in history class last month. Murdock didn't have any relatives. The legend says that right before Murdock died he came into town and tore up his deed to the mine. He said that whoever was lucky enough to find the mine could have its gold."

"As you said, we're not even sure if the mine really exists," the chief said, resuming his course for the bank.

Concord and Cody couldn't resist following. A few steps behind the chief, they entered the bank and saw a customer in front of the assayer's desk.

"It's strange that the bank has a person who writes essays full time," Cody said.

"I think assay is different from essay," Concord said.

"Right you are, Mr. Concordance!" a woman said from behind them. They turned and saw Mrs. Lavin, the manager of the bank. "An assayer is a person who analyzes substances, such as metals, to determine exactly what they are."

The boys looked back to the assayer's desk. The assayer had a large eye piece and other equipment he was using to examine a gold nugget. The customer stood in front of the desk with a bag in his hand. He didn't look like a miner at all. He was wearing an old blue cotton sweat suit. The sweatshirt had dirty forearms, and the sweat pants had so much dirt on the knees you could barely tell that the material underneath was blue. The man also wore a plain green baseball cap and torn up shoes.

"That's Mr. Morrison," Mrs. Lavin said to the Cunningham boys. "He's the one that claims to have found his gold in Murdock's Mine. That is, if it's really gold."

"Since the assayer is the one who decides whether or not the gold is real, why did you need Chief Riggins?" Concord asked quietly. He noticed that Chief Riggins was staying out of sight in the corner.

"Because a bank in a neighboring state had some gold nuggets stolen two weeks ago," Mrs. Lavin explained. "If Mr. Morrison's nuggets have the same purity percentage, it's going to be highly suspicious."

"He probably didn't figure that all the little banks would talk to each other," Cody said.

"We're not saying he's the robber yet," Mrs. Lavin said. "But it is very rare for anyone to have gold nuggets these days. The chief is here to investigate."

The assayer smiled at Mr. Morrison, stood up, and calmly walked over to Mrs. Lavin.

"It's ninety-nine-point-three percent pure," the assayer said. "That's exactly the same purity as the nuggets stolen in Elk City."

Mrs. Lavin thanked the assayer and then nodded at Chief Riggins in the corner. The chief understood the signal and walked over to Mr. Morrison.

"Mr. Morrison," the chief said, "I'd like to ask you a few questions."

Mr. Morrison jumped at the sight of a police uniform. His eyes opened wide, and then he calmed himself.

"Yes?" Mr. Morrison said.

"Where were you two weeks ago?" the chief asked.

"Why, up at Murdock's Mine," Mr. Morrison said, "mining these nuggets."

"I see," Chief Riggins said. "And how long have you been up there?"

"It's been three months," Mr. Morrison said. "I was in a plane crash up there."

"A plane crash?" Chief Riggins gasped. "We didn't hear about a plane crash."

"I know," Mr. Morrison said. "That's why no one came looking for me. I suppose I shouldn't be surprised. Nobody knew I was going on the sightseeing trip, and I took off from my own private air strip in the woods. My plane's engine stalled over the mountains north of here, and I had to crash land. Fortunately, I didn't get hurt."

"That's pretty lucky," the chief said. "How did you survive for three months in the wilderness?"

"I think that was the lucky part, really," Mr. Morrison said. "I hadn't taken anything with me because I was only planning to go sightseeing for an hour. When I crashed, my radio was destroyed, so I couldn't call for help. I was about to start hiking out when I looked to my left and saw a small opening in the mountainside."

"That must have been Murdock's Mine," Cody whispered to Concord.

"I stuck my head in the opening and saw a candle and some matches," Mr. Morrison said. "I lit the candle and crawled into the opening. It was a tunnel, and it wasn't more than a few feet tall. I had to crawl the whole way. As I worked my way in, I found a knife, a fishing pole, and other utensils. I kept crawling and eventually came to the end of the tunnel. There I found a pick ax, a canvas bag, and Murdock's diary. That's when I realized that I had found Murdock's Mine."

"So you've been mining up there ever since?" Chief Riggins asked.

"Mining and surviving," he said. "Fortunately, the tunnel didn't get very cold at night, so I slept in it under a blanket of pine branches. And I was able to catch and eat fish out of the nearby stream. After I realized that I could survive up there, I couldn't resist mining Murdock's gold. You know what Murdock said, anybody who finds the mine can have the gold. It's been a long three months, though. I came straight to the bank when I made it back to town. I can't wait to get out of these clothes."

Concord stepped forward. "Mr. Morrison, may I ask you a question?"

"Yes," he replied suspiciously.

"How did you mine gold in a tunnel so small that you couldn't even stand up in it?" he asked.

Mr. Morrison nodded. "It wasn't easy," he said. "I had to chip a little rock away, load it into the canvas bag, and drag it out of the tunnel on my hands and knees. I must have crawled in and out of that tunnel thirty times a day. It was no short tunnel, either. It was tough work."

Chief Riggins sighed and looked at Mrs. Lavin. She gestured that she didn't know what to think. Then the chief glanced at Concord. Chief Riggins' eyes brightened when he saw Concord flipping through his Bible. He knew the Scripture Sleuth was on the case.

To give Concord a little more time, Chief Riggins decided to stall. He turned back to Mr. Morrison. "You understand we'll have to check out your story," Chief Riggins said. "We can start by having you lead us to your plane wreckage."

Mr. Morrison laughed. "It's a long walk," he said. "It took me four days to hike out of there, and there's no trail."

Concord suddenly looked up and turned toward Chief

Riggins. "I don't think you need to bother, Chief," Concord said. "He was never there."

"What?" Mr. Morrison exclaimed. "Why do you say that?"

"Because of Deuteronomy 29:5," The Concordance said. "Your story has a hole in it. At least it should have."

How did Concord know Mr. Morrison was making the story up?

Read Deuteronomy 29:5 for Concord's clue.

The solution to "Murdock's Mine" is on page 79.

9

SCIENCE CLASS SURVIVAL

Science was one of Concord's favorite subjects in school. It was also his most dangerous. Concord's science teacher, Mr. Albright, loved to do spectacular science demonstrations. He thought they were the best way to excite students about science. Unfortunately, the demonstrations didn't always go as expected.

Students were still talking about the exploding helium balloon demonstration that had caught Mr. Albright's hair on fire last week. And no one could forget the pipe cleaner experiment that had sent Mr. Albright to the ear specialist last month.

Fortunately, Concord's seat assignment wasn't in the front row. But it was in the second row, which was still clearly in the danger zone.

Today Mr. Albright was introducing a lesson on chemical reactions. On one side of his lab table Mr. Albright had a bubbling jar of green liquid. On the other side was a steaming jar of red liquid.

"Mr. Albright," said John Spencer in the front row, "I feel kind of sick. May I go see the nurse?"

Lori Lindsay leaned across the aisle to whisper to Concord.

"Do you think John is faking it so he won't have to watch the experiment?" she asked.

"Could be," Concord whispered back. "But I did see him eating the burrito supreme in the cafeteria today. You never know what that'll do to you."

Mr. Albright raised his lab goggles to his forehead and looked at John. John's thick black hair made his thin face seem even more pale than it was, and his brown-rimmed glasses hung slightly crooked on his face. "You'll miss the demonstration, John," Mr. Albright said. "But I suppose if you're sick you'd better go."

John left the room, and the rest of the students in the front row immediately raised their hands, hoping the same excuse would work for them.

"You can't all be sick," Mr. Albright said. Then he smiled. "Don't worry, I know exactly what I'm doing."

The front row students looked at each other and slowly dropped their hands, except for one.

"But Mr. Albright," said Robbie Lockey, "my pen just broke and leaked ink all over my jeans. I've got an extra pair in my locker. May I go change?"

Mr. Albright walked over to Robbie and inspected. Sure enough, Robbie had huge patches of fresh ink all over his jeans. Robbie was tall and blond, and he shifted nervously in his chair while Mr. Albright and the entire class looked at his leg.

"No need to change," Mr. Albright said. "I've got a chemical that will take that right out."

"Ah, that's okay," Robbie said, fearing what might happen to his legs. "I'd rather just go change."

Mr. Albright sighed as he considered the request, and finally he allowed Robbie to leave. The teacher then resumed his introduction to the demonstration.

Lori leaned over to Concord again. "I'm surprised that Robbie didn't try to blame John for getting ink on his jeans," she whispered.

"Why's that?" Concord whispered back.

"John and Robbie are always trying to get each other into trouble," she said.

"And they both just left the class," Concord said suspiciously.

Mr. Albright finished explaining his experiment to the class. Then, just as he was preparing to pour the red chemical into the green, the fire alarm went off.

"Hey Mr. Albright," a student yelled, "the fire alarm is early. Doesn't it usually goes off right after your experiments?"

The students laughed as they made their way out of the building.

A few minutes later, Concord stood outside waiting for the fire bell to ring a second time. That was the signal that the fire alarm was only a drill, and students and teachers could then go back into the building.

But the bell wasn't ringing.

Concord then noticed that John had joined the students and teachers on the field.

"Feeling better, John?" Concord asked as he approached him.

"Not really," John said, adjusting his glasses. "I never made it to the nurse. I stopped at my locker on the way, and then the fire alarm went off."

"John Spencer!" a loud voice suddenly boomed. It was Principal Ironsides. He walked through the crowd toward John. Following Mr. Ironsides stride for stride was Robbie. "Are you responsible for this alarm, John?" Mr. Ironsides demanded.

"What?" John replied with surprise.

"This fire alarm was set off by a smoke bomb in the boys

bathroom," Mr. Ironsides said with a fierce scowl. He pulled Robbie forward. "We thought Robbie did it because he was seen leaving the bathroom right before the alarm went off. But Robbie says you did it."

John glared at Robbie, and then looked back to Principal Ironsides. "But I never went to the bathroom," he said.

Mr. Ironsides' eyes narrowed. "Mr. Albright says he sent you to see the nurse because you were sick, but the nurse says you never showed up," he said. "How do you explain that?"

"I was on my way to the nurse, but I stopped at my locker to drop off my books," John said. "Before I could get to the nurse, the alarm went off."

Concord stepped forward and caught Mr. Ironsides' eye.

"Cunningham!" Mr. Ironsides barked. "Were you a witness to this, too?"

"I saw both students leave Mr. Albright's class," Concord said. "But I don't know if either one had the smoke bomb."

Concord looked at Robbie's clean jeans. "I see you were able to change your ink-stained jeans, Robbie," he said.

"Just barely," Robbie said. "I was changing in one of the bathroom stalls when John threw his smoke bomb in the bathroom door."

Concord considered the statement. "If you were in the stall, how do you know it was John?" he asked.

Mr. Ironsides raised an eyebrow and rotated his scowl toward Robbie.

"After I made it out of the bathroom," Robbie began, "I caught a glimpse of the back of the smoke bomber's tee shirt just before he went around the corner a couple classrooms down. It said 'Born to Run' just like the back of John's shirt."

Mr. Ironsides asked John to turn around. Sure enough, on the back of John's shirt were the words "Born to Run."

Robbie turned to Mr. Ironsides. "I was lucky to make it out of the bathroom alive," he said dramatically. "The smoke made me cough like crazy, and I could barely pull up my clean pants. By the time I made it out of the bathroom, the smoke was as thick as the trees on the bottom of Mount Redhead."

As Mr. Ironsides asked the crowd if there were any other witnesses, Concord pulled his Bible out of his backpack. He turned to the concordance section and found the subject he was looking for. Then he quickly flipped to a verse.

"John should be in big trouble for this!" Robbie said as a grin of satisfaction crept across his face.

Concord shook his head. "I think you're the one that's going to be in big trouble, Robbie," he said.

Mr. Ironsides turned to Concord. "Cunningham, are you saying that Robbie is making up this story about John?" he asked.

"Actually, that's what Proverbs 10:26 is saying," The Concordance replied.

Principal Ironsides bent down and read the verse in Concord's Bible. He rubbed his chin for a moment, and then his eyes bulged. "Hmph!" he grunted. He grabbed Robbie by the elbow and took him to the office. "I hope you like cleaning bathrooms, Robbie!"

How did Concord know that Robbie was lying?

Read Proverbs 10:26 for the clue that Concord gave to Mr. Ironsides.

The solution to "Science Class Survival" is on page 80.

THE CANINE CRIMINAL

Though Concord walked home from school everyday, he rarely went the same way two days in a row. He enjoyed seeing different parts of town.

Today his route took him through the Pine Tops town square. The town square had many interesting shops, and Concord's favorite was Cobby's Hobby Shop. The shop's owner, Mr. Cobby, was one of the best model makers in the Northwest.

Since Mr. Cobby was seventy years old, he was also the last person Concord expected to see running across the town square.

"Come back here you little rascal!" Mr. Cobby yelled as he chased a small dog.

The dog had a model airplane in its mouth, but it could still run much faster than old Mr. Cobby. After about twenty steps, the shop owner was out of breath. The dog went around the corner, and Mr. Cobby went for the nearest bench.

"Mr. Cobby," Concord said as he hurried over to the bench, "what did that dog do?"

"That dog stole my Smoke Jumper-21 model," Mr. Cobby said, gasping for air.

"The new firefighting airplane?" Concord asked.

"Right," Mr. Cobby confirmed. "That model was my first wooden model of the new plane. I did it all by hand. It took me two hundred hours. I just put it on sale yesterday for seven hundred dollars."

"Do you know whose dog that was?" Concord asked.

"No," Mr. Cobby said. "He had a name tag on, though. It said 'Chipmunk.'"

"We'd better call Police Chief Riggins," Concord said.

Mr. Cobby nodded, and Concord helped him back to the hobby shop.

Chief Riggins was soon in the shop filling out a report.

"I never thought a canine criminal could cause so much trouble," the chief said. "This is Chipmunk's third theft today!"

"Do you think he's taking things at random?" Concord asked.

The chief shook his head. "It looks like he's been trained somehow," he said. "He only steals valuable stuff. He stole a rare book out of the bookstore down the street, and he stole a silver spoon collection out of the antique store."

"How does he know what to take?" Concord asked.

"We think his trainer must have rubbed something on the items that Chipmunk is supposed to steal," the chief said. "Then Chipmunk runs into a store, sniffs around, grabs whatever has the scent, and runs through the aisles with it until the door opens. Then he runs out."

Chief Riggins turned to Mr. Cobby. "Has anyone touched the Smoke Jumper-21 since you put it on sale?" he asked.

"Lots of folks have looked at it, but only two have asked me take it out of the display case," Mr. Cobby said. "Carol Jones from the bookstore wanted to take a closer look. Walter Perkins did, too."

"I doubt Chipmunk is Carol Jones' dog," the chief said. "She's allergic to dogs. In fact, she started sneezing like crazy after Chipmunk robbed her bookstore this morning. That leaves Walter Perkins."

Concord glanced out the shop window. "Chief, look!" he cried, pointing toward the street.

Chipmunk was trotting across the town square, heading straight for the jewelry store.

Chief Riggins burst out the hobby shop door and ran across the square. A customer was leaving the jewelry store, and Chipmunk was just about to slip through the open door. Chief Riggins ran up behind Chipmunk and scooped the dog into his arms.

"Gotcha!" the chief said with satisfaction.

Concord caught up just as the chief was carefully removing Chipmunk's collar and name tag. He put them in a plastic bag and said, "I'm going to take the collar and tag to headquarters for fingerprint testing. While the lab is working on that, Chipmunk and I will visit Walter Perkins."

"Mind if I come along, Chief?" Concord asked.

"Not at all," the chief said. "I could use somebody to hold the dog while I drive. Besides, having The Concordance along usually comes in handy."

After a quick stop at police headquarters, Concord, Chief Riggins, and Chipmunk drove across town to Walter Perkins' house.

When they arrived, they were greeted by another dog with a name tag that read "Duke."

"I wonder if they know each other," Chief Riggins said as he put Chipmunk down. The two dogs sniffed each other, as dogs usually do. Then they began to play with each other, but they gave no signs that they knew each other.

Chief Riggins picked up Chipmunk and went to the front door of the house. Concord followed him onto the porch.

The chief rang the doorbell, and Mr. Perkins came to the door. Mr. Perkins was about fifty years old. He wore a flannel shirt and black pants, and he looked like he had just awakened.

"Good afternoon, Mr. Perkins," Chief Riggins said.

"Afternoon?" Mr. Perkins said with a yawn.

"I hope we didn't wake you," the chief said.

"It's okay," Mr. Perkins said. "I suppose it's time to get up anyway."

"Have you been asleep long?" Concord asked.

"Since five o'clock this morning," Mr. Perkins replied. "I was up all night working on crossword puzzles."

Mr. Perkins looked at Chipmunk and then back to the chief with a curious look.

"I was wondering if this dog is yours," the chief said, petting Chipmunk.

"Nope," Mr. Perkins said.

"Do you know whose he is?" Concord asked.

"Never seen him," Mr. Perkins replied.

Concord looked back to Chipmunk to see if he was reacting to Mr. Perkins. Chipmunk didn't seem to be acting any different.

The chief put Chipmunk down and took out a notepad. Chipmunk ran into the yard.

"Mr. Perkins, were you in Cobby's Hobby Shop yesterday?" the chief asked.

"Yes," Mr. Perkins said, yawning again. "I was in there checking out the new Smoke Jumper-21 model. It's a dandy."

"Are you aware that the Smoke Jumper-21 model was stolen today?" the chief asked.

"Stolen?" Mr. Perkins said with a surprised expression. "That's terrible. I wanted to go back and take another look at it. It's one of a kind you know."

"So I hear," the chief said.

Mr. Perkins glanced out at his yard. "Hey!" he yelled.

Chipmunk had tipped over a trash can and was starting to rummage through the trash. Mr. Perkins looked back at Chief Riggins with a scowl.

"Thanks a lot, Chief," Mr. Perkins said. He grabbed his boots off the porch and began to put them on.

"I'm sorry, Mr. Perkins," the chief said as he blushed with embarrassment. "I wouldn't have thought that little dog could tip over that trash can."

"Well he just did," Mr. Perkins said angrily. "He should have been named Racoon instead of Chipmunk. I get racoons digging through my trash all the time." He finished tying his boot laces. "I'd better go clean that mess up."

"I wanted to ask you a few more questions," Chief Riggins said.

Mr. Perkins shook his head. "If I don't clean up that trash right away, Duke will go over there and start digging through it, too. Then we'll have a really big mess."

Concord's eyes flashed to the side. Then he turned to Mr. Perkins. "I think you've gotten yourself into a big mess already, Mr. Perkins."

"What?" Mr. Perkins asked, irritated.

"What?" Chief Riggins asked, confused.

"Mr. Perkins hasn't been telling us the truth, Chief," Concord said.

"How do you know?" Chief Riggins asked.

"It's right in the Bible," The Concordance announced. He pulled his Bible out of his backpack and turned to the New Testament. He flipped a few pages to the left and put his finger on a verse. "Here, Chief," Concord said as he handed him the Bible. "Read John 10:3. You'll see that Mr. Perkins has some explaining to do."

How did Concord know that Mr. Perkins had been lying?

Read John 10:3 to find the clue that Concord gave the chief.

The solution to "The Canine Criminal" is on page 81.

11

FOOTBALL FRAUD

The Cunningham family sat shocked in the football field stands. The Pine Tops High School football team had just lost the game 21-0. Losing was never fun. But to lose to cross-county rival Clearwater High School made it even worse.

"Weren't we supposed to win this game by 20 or 30 points?" Concord asked his dad.

"That's what everybody said," Mr. Cunningham replied as he screwed the lid on his thermos. "I don't understand it. It's like Clearwater High knew every play we were going to run before we ran it."

"I hope Cody isn't too upset," Mrs. Cunningham said. Concord's older brother was a wide receiver for Pine Tops. "He didn't make a single catch."

"How could he?" Mr. Cunningham replied. "Clearwater's players seemed to know every play he was going to run."

"Hey dad," Concord said as he gazed at the field, "why do you think Chief Riggins is talking to the referee?"

Mr. Cunningham scanned the field until he spotted Chief Riggins. The chief showed his police radio to the referee and then pointed at Mount Redhead. The referee pulled his white hat off his head and began to rub his chin.

"Maybe we should check it out," Mr. Cunningham said as

his reporter instincts awakened.

"You two can do that," Mrs. Cunningham said, "and Charlotte and I will head home." She knew Mr. Cunningham's investigation could take a while.

The family agreed, and Concord and his dad made their way to Chief Riggins and the referee. The chief saw them approaching.

"Good evening, Cunninghams," Chief Riggins said with a grin.

"Not so good for the home team," Mr. Cunningham said.

"It's about to get better," the chief replied with a wink.

Concord and his dad looked at each other in confusion.

Chief Riggins turned back to Referee Lewis Fite. "Are you ready to head up there?" he asked.

"Sure thing," the tall, slender referee said.

"What's going on, Chief?" Mr. Cunningham asked.

"We're heading up to the Mount Redhead Observatory," Chief Riggins said.

"You mean the building with the huge telescope?" Concord asked.

"That's right," the chief replied.

"What does the observatory have to do with tonight's football game?" Mr. Cunningham asked.

"That huge telescope is supposed to observe the stars, but tonight it may have been observing this football game instead," Chief Riggins replied.

"But that's not against the rules," Mr. Cunningham replied.

"But spying on the plays in the Pine Tops play book is," the chief said.

Referee Fite explained, "Chief Riggins thinks the telescope may have been zoomed in on the Pine Tops coach's play book during tonight's game."

Mr. Cunningham's jaw dropped. It all made sense. The telescope could zoom in on the play book and tell the Clearwater High coaches what plays Pine Tops was going to run. That's how Clearwater always knew just what to do. And that's how they could beat a team that was far superior to them.

"Can that telescope read a play book all the way from Mount Redhead?" Concord asked.

"It sure could," Mr. Cunningham replied. He had done a newspaper story on the observatory not too long ago, and he remembered the magnification power of the huge telescope.

"But how would the telescope operator tell the Clearwater coaches what he saw?" Concord asked.

"All it takes is two of these," Mr. Cunningham said as he held up his cell phone. "The information could be relayed instantly."

"That's actually what tipped us off to this scheme," Chief Riggins said. "One of our police radios accidentally picked up the cell phone conversation. We heard the plays being relayed to the Clearwater coaches. At halftime, one of the Clearwater coaches asked the man on the other end how the weather was up on Mount Redhead. The man said it was nippy up there. That's when we figured out that the informant was on Mount Redhead, and we knew he had to be using the telescope."

"Do you know who's on duty up there tonight?" Mr. Cunningham asked.

"That's what Referee Fite and I are about to find out," the chief replied.

Mr. Cunningham knew a big story when he heard one. "What happens if this turns out to be true?" he asked Referee Fite.

"Clearwater High will be forced to forfeit the game due to

cheating," Referee Fite replied.

Mr. Cunningham turned to Concord. "Ready to take a ride?"

"You bet!" Concord exclaimed.

"Then let's get to the car," Mr. Cunningham said. He turned back to the chief and Referee Fite. "We'll meet you up there!"

The observatory was halfway up the side of Mount Redhead. Though astronomers would have preferred to have the observatory on the top of the mountain, roads couldn't be built that high due to the steepness of the peak. In fact, just driving halfway up the mountain was a curvy and treacherous ride.

"Good thing Mom isn't with us," Concord said as they banked into a turn.

"Yeah, she's never liked this road," Mr. Cunningham agreed. "especially when I'm driving. It makes her carsick."

Concord put his hand on his stomach. "I know what she means."

After a few more turns and a close call with a deer, the Cunninghams' car followed the tail lights of Chief Riggins' patrol car and Referee Fite's pickup into the observatory parking lot.

The observatory was a small, perfectly round building with a dome on top. The dome's motorized panels had been opened, and the telescope was aimed at the stars.

"Let's see who's home," Chief Riggins said as he led the group from the parking lot into the observatory.

Inside, two men stood near the telescope. A tall man in a white lab coat stepped forward.

"I'm Dr. Gordon Griff," he said. "I'm the chief astronomer on duty tonight. This is my assistant, Reece." Reece was a middle-aged volunteer in a tee shirt and a baseball cap.

While everyone exchanged handshakes, Concord surveyed the facility. There was only one room, with the telescope in the center. The telescope's eyepiece was about 6 feet above the ground. There was a platform next to the eyepiece with a ladder dropping down to the side. Concord couldn't tell exactly where the telescope was pointed. He knew, however, that if it had been focused on the football field earlier, it had certainly been moved.

The only other piece of equipment in the room was a computer next to the telescope.

Since the observatory was a round, one-room building, the wall was one continuous curve. It was painted like outer space, complete with planets, the moon, and even a nebula.

"Are you here for a tour?" Dr. Griff asked the group.

"Actually, we're here to ask you about what you've been observing tonight," Chief Riggins said.

Mr. Cunningham pulled out his reporter's notebook and began to take notes.

Dr. Griff swallowed hard and glanced at Reece. "Just the usual," he said. "A planet here, a comet there, and a few asteroids in between."

"And have you been doing all the telescope work tonight, Dr. Griff, or has Reece been operating the telescope as well?" Referee Fite asked.

"Just me," Dr. Griff said. "Only chief astronomers are allowed to operate the telescope because it's so expensive." Referee Fite looked over at Reece, who nodded in agreement.

"Why do you ask?" Dr. Griff questioned.

"We overheard a cell phone call coming from Mount Redhead, describing the plays being chosen from the Pine Tops High School play book during tonight's football game," Chief Riggins explained. "We believe that you used the telescope to help Clearwater High cheat."

Dr. Griff raised his voice and protested, "You're accusing me of helping a football team cheat?"

"Dr. Griff," Mr. Cunningham asked, "do you have any kids who attend Clearwater High?"

"Reece and I both do," Dr. Griff said as he put his hands on his hips. "But that doesn't mean we helped the school's football team cheat."

There was a pause in the conversation. Then Chief Riggins had a thought.

"Do your computers record what the telescope views?" the chief asked.

"They do," Dr. Griff said as his eyes narrowed. "But the computers haven't been working tonight. I'm afraid they haven't recorded anything."

"Is that true, Reece?" Chief Riggins asked.

Reece looked over at Dr. Griff as he tried to decide what to say.

"Uh, yeah," Reece said. His foot twitched nervously. "In fact, the computers have been so messed up that they gave Dr. Griff a huge headache. He had to go lean against the wall in the corner for at least an hour to clear his mind."

Dr. Griff nodded. "That's right. It was a terrible headache."

"And how do you explain the cell phone call that came from up here, which gave Clearwater High the plays?" Referee Fite asked.

Dr. Griff smirked. "Did you say the call was from the observatory, or just from Mount Redhead in general?" he asked.

"Hmm," Chief Riggins murmured. "I suppose it wasn't exactly clear where on Mount Redhead the caller was."

"So, it really could have been anyone," Dr. Griff said.

Off to the side, Concord had been flipping through his

Bible. Something about what he heard hadn't made sense, and now he knew exactly what it was.

Concord stepped forward. "I'm afraid one of these men didn't think his story through," Concord proclaimed. "Dr. Griff and Reece are lying about the computers giving Dr. Griff a headache."

"And what makes you say that?" Dr. Griff asked. "Having computer problems can easily give you a headache. And then you just have to take a break and relax."

All eyes turned to Concord.

"You'd better read Acts 26:26," the Concordance said as he held out his Bible. "Something that didn't happen in that verse couldn't have happen here."

How did Concord know that Dr. Griff and Reece were lying?

Read Acts 26:26 for the clue that Concord gave the group.

The solution to "Football Fraud" is on page 82.

12

Sauna Surprise

Concord and Charlie raced their bikes down a forest road.

"Do you think we'll be the only ones there?" Charlie asked as they rounded a curve.

"I hope not," Concord replied. "It's always nice when somebody already has the fire going."

The boys were biking to a special cave just outside of Pine Tops known as the Sauna Cave.

A few moments later, their bikes rolled to a stop in front of the cave's mountainside entrance. Before entering, Charlie looked about twenty five feet up the mountain and saw a column of smoke rising through the trees. It was coming from a hole in the ceiling of the cave. "Yes!" he exclaimed. "It looks there's a fire already going."

They dismounted their bikes and entered the cave.

The entrance was a tunnel about five feet long and as wide as a door. After the tunnel, the cave widened into a large room. Spring water cascaded down one of the cave's walls into a small pool.

The cave had been transformed into a sauna years ago by lumberjacks who needed a place to ease their aching muscles. They had built a large fire ring in the center of the cave, directly under a hole in the ceiling, which allowed smoke to escape. Once a good fire had burnt for awhile, the lumberjacks would throw large rocks into the embers.

After a few minutes, they would scoop the red-hot rocks

out of the fire, place them on the dirt floor, and pour spring water on them. Steam would then radiate off the rocks and fill the cave, making it a sauna.

The old practice had never died. Pine Tops locals frequently went to the sauna cave when they were sore, had a cold, or just wanted to relax.

Or, in the case of Concord and Charlie, they went when they were hungry.

"Got the hot dogs?" Charlie asked as he got off his bike.

"Yep," Concord replied as he tapped his backpack.

"Got the sticks?" Concord asked.

"Sure do," Charlie replied as he untied them from the frame of his bike.

Not many people realized that the sauna cave also had the best hot dog roasting fire in the area. Since the fire would burn for hours at a time, it created a glowing sea of embers that were ideal for roasting the perfect hot dog.

When the boys entered the cave they were greeted by an elderly Pine Tops couple. Mr. and Mrs. Walker were wearing shorts and tee shirts, and they were sitting in lawn chairs next to one of the cave's five bowling ball-sized, steaming rocks.

"Hi boys," Mr. Walker said. "Here for a little steam?"

"Actually, we're here for a little lunch," Concord replied as he dropped his backpack to the ground and pulled out the hot dogs.

Mrs. Walker smiled. "Have at it," she said. "I was just telling George that we should have brought some marshmallows."

Concord and Charlie looked at each other, wondering why they had never thought of that.

Then Charlie looked down at the deep pile of embers. "Looks like a real nice fire," he said. "We can start roasting right away."

"We've had the fire burning for a couple hours now," Mr. Walker said. "We both have arthritis, and the steam works wonders on our joints."

"Well, hot dogs work wonders on our stomachs," Charlie joked.

The group laughed.

Concord knelt down to his backpack and pulled out a pocketknife.

Charlie handed him two sticks, and Concord quickly whittled a sharp point at the end of each.

Meanwhile, Mr. Walker hobbled over to a shovel leaning against the cave wall. Then he scooped up a rock and put it in the fire.

"Steam's getting a little thin," he said. "Another hot rock ought to do the trick." He sat back down and waited for the fire to heat the rock.

While the elderly couple rested in their lawn chairs, Concord and Charlie roasted and ate one hot dog after another. Before long, the whole package was gone!

"Do you boys have a stomach ache yet?" Mrs. Walker asked with a chuckle.

"I don't know about Charlie, but I was full two hot dogs ago," Concord said. The two boys and Mrs. Walker laughed. But Mr. Walker stared out the cave's entrance with a straight face.

"What's the matter, George?" Mrs. Walker asked. "Were you hoping for a hot dog, too?"

"Not me," Mr. Walker said. Then he pointed out the cave entrance. "But I think he might have been."

The group looked out the cave's entrance and froze in scared silence. About fifty yards away was a grizzly bear, sniffing the wind.

"Uh-oh," Charlie whispered. "What do we do?"

"Let's just hope he doesn't figure out where the smell of hot dogs came from," Mrs. Walker whispered back.

"I don't think we'll be that lucky," Mr. Walker replied. "Grizzlies have a keen sense of smell. He'll probably figure it out pretty quick."

"Then what do we do?" Mrs. Walker asked.

Concord's eyes started darting back and forth as he considered the situation.

"Can we block the cave's entrance?" Charlie asked.

"With what?" the Mrs. Walker asked.

"How about firewood ," Charlie said.

"We're down to our last piece of wood," Mr. Walker said as he pointed to a small log beside the fire.

"Should we make a run for it?" Charlie asked.

"You're never supposed to run from bears," Concord replied. "They might chase you, and they can easily outrun you."

Mrs. Walker looked up at the hole in the cave's ceiling. "What about escaping through the vent?" Mrs. Walker asked.

"There's no way to get up there," Mr. Walker replied. The vent was about twenty five feet above them. There was no rope, ladder, or anything else in the cave to help them reach the vent.

Suddenly, Concord ran over to the cave's wall and grabbed the shovel. "I've got it!" he said.

Mr. Walker shook his head as Concord walked towards the fire. He thought he knew what Concord was about to do. "Young man," Mr. Walker said, "if you think that filling this cave with steam is going to prevent the bear from seeing us, it's not going to work. His nose will still bring him in here looking for food. And when he discovers that the hot dogs are all gone, the food might just might turn out to be us!"

"Actually, I'm not going to steam anything," Concord said.

"Then what are you going to do?" Mrs. Walker asked. "Are you going to try to beat him with a shovel? He'll snap it in two!"

"Nope," Concord replied as he stood next to the fire. "I've got a better idea." He quickly reached over to his backpack, pulled out his Bible, and handed it to Mr. Walker. "Read Proverbs 6:28. You'll see what I'm doing."

How will Concord save the group from the bear?

Read Proverbs 6:28 for the clue that Concord gave Mr. Walker.

The solution to "Sauna Surprise" is on page 83.

Solutions

Solution to Chapter One: The Roller Play

Judges 16:9 describes a string being snapped when it comes into contact with a flame. Rodney snapped the rope by burning through it. He hid behind the tower so no one could see him. Then he lit the end of the broom handle on fire (Mr. Ironsides must not have found all of Rodney's matches earlier in the day). Rodney held the long broom handle up to the rope until the flame burned through it. Once the rope snapped, he pulled down the broom and blew out the flame.

But he couldn't hide all the evidence. The end of the broom handle had become black from burning, and some of the soot had rubbed off on Rodney's hand when he tried to cover it.

Rodney didn't get detention for the rest of his life, as Abby had wished. However, Mr. Ironsides made him clean the cafeteria for two months, which was just as bad.

Solution to Chapter Two: The Soccer Ball Surprise

Genesis 7:17-18 explains how Noah's ark floated on the surface of the water as the water level rose in the flood. Concord realized that the soccer ball would float, too. By filling the hole with water, the soccer ball would rise to the surface of the ground.

Concord asked Mr. Wicks to keep the water running through the hose for a couple extra minutes so he could fill the hole. Mr. Wicks agreed, and the soccer ball soon floated to the top of the hole.

Since Concord had figured out how to get the ball out of the hole, his team was declared the winner of the soccer game. However, Concord and his teammates agreed it would be more fun to finish the game on the field, so everyone decided to meet for a tiebreaker game the next day.

Solution to Chapter Three: The Bollywonk Cookbook

Acts 2:8 mentions different people having different native languages. Concord realized that the Burley twins would not have been able to communicate well enough with the Bollywonks to do all of the things they claimed.

The twins claimed that they were the first people outside of the Bollywonk tribe to meet the Bollywonks. Therefore, the twins and the Bollywonks would be speaking different languages. Besides having trouble talking to the Bollywonks, the twins would not have been able to understand the recipes on the tree, especially since they included detailed instructions.

The Burley twins were forced to admit that they had made up the cookbooks, and the cafeteria then had a sudden run on the meatloaf.

Solution to Chapter Four: The Sasquatch Snapshot

Matthew 24:27 compares lightning to the return of Christ. Concord realized that lightning is what causes thunder. When Mr. Cutler said that an extremely close thunderclap occurred above him, he forgot that lightning would have flashed almost simultaneously. Because it was so close, this lightening would have provided a moment of light in the darkness. Since Mr. Cutler claimed his camera's shutter was open at the time, there should have been much more light on the photograph.

When confronted with this fact, Mr. Cutler ran out of the office. The *Ponderosa Press* never heard from him again.

Solution to Chapter Five: Survivalist Stickup

Isaiah 7:20 refers to shaving off a beard. Concord realized that if Mr. Cosgrove had really been up in the mountains for a week, he should have had fairly long whiskers growing. Mr. Cosgrove hadn't taken a razor, or even a knife, to shave with. However, Concord noticed that Mr. Cosgrove's face was "smooth as silk" when he put on his sunburn lotion.

When confronted with the evidence of Isaiah 7:20, Mr. Cosgrove had no choice but to admit that he hadn't been on Mount Redhead all week, and he was eventually proven guilty of robbing the dump.

Solution to Chapter Six: The Sweatshirt Switcheroo

Genesis 27:27 tells of Isaac smelling the clothing of his son in order to identify him. Concord realized that if he smelled the two sweatshirts, one of them would smell like smoke. This would identify Charlotte's sweatshirt. She had been wearing her sweatshirt all evening, and when she sat by the campfire the smoke kept following her.

Only Charlotte's sweatshirt would smell like smoke because Becky had never been by the fire. Becky said that when she got back from the night hike the campfire was already out.

When Concord smelled the two sweatshirts, he discovered that the stained sweatshirt turned out to be Charlotte's. Fortunately, Mrs. Cunningham is an expert stain remover. She managed to get the stain out with some warm water and hair spray.

Solution to Chapter Seven: Locker Talk

1 Corinthians 14:7 says that people can't know what tune a flute or harp is playing if there isn't a distinction in the notes. The same rule would apply to a simple coach's whistle like Mr. Russell's. Listeners would only hear the same note being played over and over. It wouldn't sound like a song. When Bernie blew the whistle, he would hear the song in his mind, but to Bart it wouldn't sound like a song at all.

If Bart was lucky, he might be able to pick out the beat of one or two songs, but the others would just sound like a whistle blowing.

Sure enough, Bart failed the test after school.

Mr. Russell discovered that Bernie had borrowed his whistle without permission and made him run 15 laps.

Solution to Chapter Eight: Murdock's Mine

Deuteronomy 29:5 refers to the Israelites' clothing not wearing out during their forty years in the desert. Concord realized that if Mr. Morrison had been crawling on his knees through a mountain tunnel thirty times a day for three months, the soft cotton sweats certainly would have had big holes in the knees. Instead, as Concord observed when he first saw Mr. Morrison, the sweat pants were muddy but the knees were still intact. Mr. Morrison said he hadn't taken anything with him on his trip, and he had come straight to the Pine Tops bank from the wilderness, so he couldn't have changed his clothes.

Mr. Morrison had merely smeared dirt on himself so he would appear to have been mining. The only place he had found gold was the bank in the neighboring state, and he was soon serving a long prison term for robbery.

Solution to Chapter Nine: Science Class Survival

Proverbs 10:26 mentions smoke getting in the eyes. Concord realized that Robbie could not have read the back of the smoke bomber's shirt as he claimed. Robbie said that the smoke in the bathroom was thick enough to make him "cough like crazy" while he tried to pull up his clean pants. If this had been true, his eyes certainly would have been watering from the smoke (and the coughing). And with watering eyes when he came out of the bathroom, Robbie could not have read the back of a shirt that was two class-rooms away.

Caught in his lie, Robbie confessed to being the smoke bomber. Mr. Ironsides ordered him to clean the smoke bombed bathroom for the next two months.

Solution to Chapter Ten: The Canine Criminal

John 10:3 refers to a watchman calling his own sheep by name. Mr. Perkins' knew Chipmunk's name, but he shouldn't have.

Mr. Perkins claimed that this was the first time he had ever seen Chipmunk. However, after Chipmunk knocked the trash can over, Mr. Perkins complained that Chipmunk was misnamed. He said the dog "should have been named Racoon instead of Chipmunk."

Chipmunk's name tag had been removed and taken to the police station. Neither Concord nor Chief Riggins had called Chipmunk by name in front of Mr. Perkins. And, if Mr. Perkins had really been asleep all day, he wouldn't have heard anybody talking about Chipmunk's crimes.

Since Mr. Perkins knew Chipmunk's name, he had to be lying.

Mr. Perkins confessed that Chipmunk was his dog. Chief Riggins arrested Mr. Perkins, and all of the stolen items were returned (and they smelled like steak sauce).

Solution to Chapter Eleven: Football Fraud

Acts 26:26 states that something was "not done in a corner." Reece had claimed that Dr. Griff leaned against the wall in the corner to relieve a headache. Concord realized this was impossible. The observatory was a round building with a continuously curving wall. There was no corner to lean against!

Caught in Reece's lie, both men eventually confessed to using the telescope to help Clearwater High win the football game. Referee Fite immediately declared that Clearwater High forfeited the game due to cheating, and Mr. Cunningham had a front page story.

Solution to Chapter Twelve: Sauna Surprise

Proverbs 6:28 indicates that a man cannot walk on hot coals without scorching his feet. Concord realized that the same would be true of a bear.

Concord grabbed the shovel so he could scoop the glowing embers from the fire and scatter them across the floor of the entrance tunnel. That way, the bear wouldn't be able to walk inside. Sure enough, the bear took one step into the tunnel and immediately jumped back with a roar as his paw hit a hot ember. Before too long, the bear gave up and wandered away.

To show their appreciation, the Walkers bought Concord and Charlie a month's supply of hot dogs.

Concord's
Secret

If your Bible has a Concordance, it will usually be found at the back of the book. It is a collection of the most common words found in the Bible, with their most used examples in the text under the word. Sometimes there is a brief description of what the word means. Learning how to use a Concordance gives a Bible scholar a marvelous tool for finding God's Truth on any subject in His Holy Word.

Below are a few examples of words found in the Concordance. Read them for practice, look up the verses, and you will see how much fun it is to do your own Scripture Sleuthing. Then get your Bible and you will be able to solve your own mysteries in life.

Appearance - brightness, radiance, sight
I Samuel 16:7, man looks at the outward *appearance*
Matthew 6:16, for they neglect their *appearance*
Matthew 28:3, his *appearance* was like lightning

Friend -
Proverbs 17:17, a *friend* loves at all times
Proverbs 18:24, a *friend* who sticks closer than a brother
John 15:13, lay down his life for his *friend(s)*

Impossible -
Matthew 19:26, with men this is *impossible*
Luke 1:37, nothing will be *impossible* with God

Money - gain
Ecclesiastes 5:10, who loves *money* will not be satisfied
Mark 6:8, no *money* in their belt
I Timothy 3:3, free from the love of *money*
Luke 19:23, why ....not put the *money*.....bank

Parents -
Matthew 10:21, children will rise up against *parents*
Romans 1:30, disobedient to *parents*
Ephesians 6:1, children, obey your *parents*

Sword -
Genesis 3:24, flaming *sword* which turned
Psalm 57:4, their tongue, a sharp *sword*
Ephesians 6:17, the *sword* of the spirit
Proverbs 5:4, sharp as a two-edged *sword*

Glad -
Matthew 5:12, rejoice and be *glad*
Proverbs 10:1, wise son makes a father *glad*
2 Corinthians 11:19, bear with the foolish *gladly*

Serpent -
Genesis 3:1, Now the *serpent* was more crafty
Psalm 58:4, venom of a *serpent*
John 3:14, Moses lifted up the *serpent* in the wilderness.
Matthew 10:16, be shrewd as *serpents*

Trouble - distress, affliction
I Kings 20:7, see how this man is looking for *trouble*
Job 5:6, does *trouble* sprout from the ground?
Psalm 9:9, a stronghold in times of *trouble*
Proverbs 10:10, who winks the eye causes *trouble*

If you have enjoyed solving the mysteries along with Concord Cunningham, you may wish to read

Concord Cunningham:
The Scripture Sleuth
ISBN 1-885904-19-3

The Scripture Sleuth 2:
Concord Cunningham Returns
ISBN 1-885904-25-8

The Scripture Sleuth 3:
Concord Cunningham On The Case
ISBN 1-885904-39-8

The Scripture Sleuth 4:
Concord Cunningham Coast to Coast
ISBN 1-885904-53-3

Visit the Scripture Sleuth website at
www.scripturesleuth.com

For other biblical titles from Focus Publishing visit
www.focuspublishing.com